A Sweet Christmas on Sesame Street

A SCRATCH & SNIFF STORY

By Jodie Shepherd

Illustrated by Tom Brannon

Random House 🏠 New York

© 2018 Sesame Workshop®, Sesame Street®, and associated characters, trademarks, and design elements are owned and licensed by Sesame Workshop. All Rights Reserved. Published in the United States by Random House Children's Books, a division of Penguin Random House LLC, 1745 Broadway, New York, NY 10019, and in Canada by Penguin Random House Canada Limited, Toronto, in conjunction with Sesame Workshop.
Random House and the colophon are registered trademarks of Penguin Random House LLC.
Visit us on the Web! rhcbooks.com
SesameStreetBooks.com
www.sesamestreet.org
ISBN 978-0-525-58133-8
MANUFACTURED IN CHINA   10 9 8 7 6 5 4 3 2 1

Cookie Monster was walking along Sesame Street. His nose twitched. His tummy rumbled. His mouth watered. "What me body trying to tell me?" he wondered. "Oh, me know! Something dee-licious nearby."

He followed his nose to a place crowded with pine trees.
"Hi, Cookie," called a friendly voice. It was Big Bird. "Does this look like a good tree for the Christmas party?"

Cookie Monster sniffed the tall tree. "Yup! It smell good enough to eat!" he said. "Me think it just right for party."

Christmas **TREES**

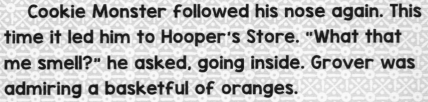

Cookie Monster followed his nose again. This time it led him to Hooper's Store. "What that me smell?" he asked, going inside. Grover was admiring a basketful of oranges.

"Cute and adorable oranges are the perfect party food, are they not?" said Grover.

"And don't forget mangoes," added Rosita.

MANGOES

MANGOES

Cookie Monster followed his nose some more to the steps of 123 Sesame Street. Bert and Ernie were sitting next to a box of candy canes. "We're going to hang these candy canes on the tree," explained Bert.

"And strings of cranberries, too," added Ernie.

"Nice decorations," Cookie said, sitting down beside them. "Me help. Me put one berry on string, three berries in tummy. . . ."

Elmo, Abby, and Julia came to the party. "We made this gingerbread house specially for the party," Abby said proudly. "Oooh," said Cookie, sniffing. "That super-duper idea. Me take closer look . . . and closer . . . and maybe closer. . . ."
"COOKIE!" cried Elmo. "No tasting!"

"I brought some spectacular things to share," Oscar the Grouch announced.

"What spectacular?" asked Cookie. "Me only smell rotten banana peels and stinky cheese."

"Exactly!" Oscar answered. "Spectacularly yucky! Heh-heh."

"Eeww!" said Abby.

The party was great! There were games to play,
Christmas carols to sing, toasty hot chocolate to sip,
and yummy food all around.

"Don't forget marshmallows!" Cookie said, adding one to his cocoa mug. "They a sometime food, and Christmas definitely happen sometime!"

"Good smells, good tastes, good friends!" Cookie exclaimed.
"What more a monster need for terrific Christmas?"
"Merry Christmas to all!" Elmo exclaimed.
"And to all, a good bite!" said Cookie. *"Nom nom nom!"*